This is to declare that

_____

is a

Certified True Fairy

with all the love and fairy magic herein.

Certified by

Talula Shimmerwing
Queen of the Fairies

The Best Kind of Fairy

by Talula Shimmerwing,
Queen of the Fairies

IN THE COMPANY OF FAIRIES

For my wonderful Fairy Godmother, with bouquets of gratitude for teaching me how to paint with rainbows.

ISBN-13 978-0-9959360-0-3

companyoffairies.com

To learn about Talula Shimmerwing or to find out how to meet the Queen of the Fairies, please visit:

talulashimmerwing.com

Tula loved to jump on the flowers.

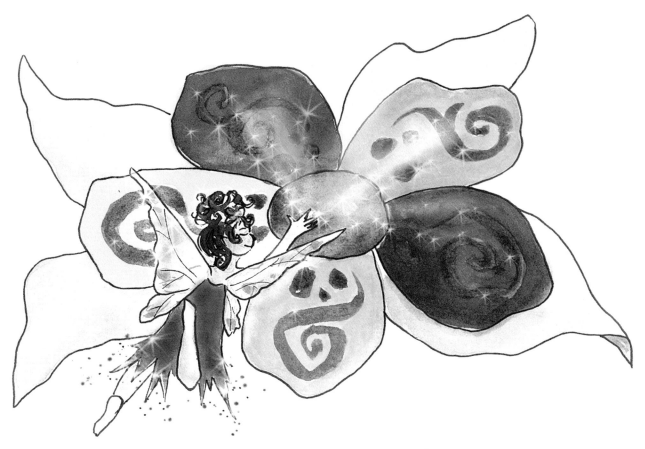

She loved to make the flowers bright colours.

She loved dancing with her friends at the Fairy Ball.

But Tula didn't like clearing out weeds at ALL.

"I just don't want to do it anymore!" she said to her friends, Sunblossom and Rosalie.

"I've been clearing out weeds day after day, and it's slow and no fun. Maybe..." Tula thought a moment, "maybe I could be another kind of fairy."

The clouds shimmered in many colours. "It's the Rainbow
Fairies!" she said. "Oh, I want to be a Rainbow Fairy."
And up she flew, all the way to the top of the clouds.

Rainbow Fairies gathered
raindrops and sunbeams and
stirred them into a large
golden pot.

"Hi! I'm Pinky!" said a fairy with hair that kept changing colour.

Pinky gave Tula some rainbow potion.

"Mmmmm..." Tula said, "it tastes like mango and vanilla."

Suddenly, rainbows shot out from her fingertips.

"Send them up, Tula!" Pinky said.

Tula sent rainbows across the sky.

That's not what rainbows look like!" The head rainbow-making
fairy said.
"At home, the flowers can look how I want," Tula thought.
"Maybe there's a better kind of fairy."

Tula gazed at the Forest of Dreams that glowed with golden-green magic below.

"It's the Forestsong Fairies! Oh, I want to be a Forestsong Fairy," she said.

Tula flew down to the largest tree. Around her, fairies played
and whispered to the trees.
"Trees like to be sung to," a Forestsong Fairy named Aspen said.

Aspen taught Tula a Tree Song.
"Green and strong, bright and true.
Grow, beautiful tree, because I love you."
The tree hummed and grew taller and bigger.

But it was windy up in the treetops. Tula's wings were wider than those of the Forestsong Fairies, and the wind blew her off a tree. OUCH!

"That wouldn't happen at home," Tula grumbled. "Maybe there's a better kind of fairy."

Tula flew to a silvery pool in a glade. She saw glimmering shapes moving in the depths.

"It's the Seashimmer Fairies! Oh, I want to be a Seashimmer Fair she said.

The pool magically opened into a vast underwater sea.

A Seashimmer Fairy named Nemony placed a blue jewel at Tula's throat.

"You'll need this to breathe," she said. "Follow me!"

Tula swam as fast as she could with the Seashimmer Fairies through underwater palaces that gleamed like mother of pearl.

But she didn't have webbed feet and hands, like the Seashimmer Fairies did. They were much faster.

"Hurry up, Tula!" they called.
"It's more fun to fly," Tula thought. "Maybe there's
a better kind of fairy."

Tula flew towards the Crystal Mountains.
She saw a glow coming from a cave.

"It's the Crystalmist Fairies! Oh, I want to be a
Crystalmist Fairy," she said.

Tula flew inside, into a cavern
full of glowing crystals.

"Crystals make any type of
magic stronger," a Crystalmist
Fairy named Jaden said. "We
send them to fairies all over the
Fairy Lands."
"That looks fun!" Tula said.

But it was chilly in the caves. BRRRRRR.

Tula missed the flowers and sunshine back home, and her friends. She thought of all the places she had been – each had something she loved, but none were just right. What if there was no place for her?

Then Tula had an idea.

"Will a crystal make weeding go faster?"
she asked.

"Yes, try this one." and Jaden gave her a green emerald.

"Oooh, thanks!" Tula said. "Maybe it would be fun to be a
Flowerdance Fairy after all."

So Tula flew back to the Flower Hills and found...

...her garden was overgrown with weeds!
Great Spotted Ladybugs!

Tula used her new green crystal, and cleared them out so fast,
she even had time to help her friends before the Fairy Ball began.

Tula showed her friends the green crystal, the bottle of rainbow potion, the blue jewel, and sang them the Tree Song.

"You're an Everything Fairy!" Sunblossom and Rosalie said.
Tula grinned. "That's the BEST kind of fairy!!"

What kind of fairy are YOU? Draw it here:

Made in the USA
Monee, IL
19 August 2020